THE GIRL THE FISH
& THE CROWN

A Spanish Folktale

Adapted and illustrated by

MARILEE HEYER

VIKING

Once upon a time there lived, on the bank of a river, a man and a woman who had a daughter. As she was an only child, and very pretty besides, they never could make up their minds to punish her for her faults or to teach her nice manners. And as for work—she laughed in her mother's face if she asked her to help cook the dinner or to wash the plates. All the girl would do was spend her days in dancing and playing with her friends. For any use she was to her parents, they might as well have had no daughter at all.

One morning her mother looked so tired that even the selfish girl could not help seeing it, and asked if there was anything she might do, so that her mother could rest a little.

The good woman looked so surprised and grateful for this offer that the girl felt rather ashamed, and at that moment would have scrubbed the house from ceiling to floor if she had been requested. But her mother only begged her to take the fishing net out to the bank of the river and mend some holes in it, as her father intended to go fishing that night.

The girl took the net and worked so hard that soon there was not a hole to be found. She felt very pleased with herself, and she had plenty to amuse her, as everybody who passed by stopped to have a chat with her. Now the sun was high overhead, and she was just folding her net to carry it home when she heard a loud splash behind her. Looking around, she saw a big fish jump into the air. She seized the net and flung it into the water where the circles were spreading one behind the other, and, more by luck than skill, drew out the fish.

"Well, you *are* a beauty!" she cried.

The fish looked up at her and said, "You had better not kill me, for if you do, I will turn you into a fish yourself!"

The girl laughed scornfully, and ran straight in to her mother.

"Look what I have caught," she said gaily. "But it is almost a pity to eat it, for it can talk, and it declares that, if I kill it, it will turn me into a fish."

"Oh, put it back, put it back!" implored her mother. "Perhaps it is skilled in magic. Your father and I would die from grief if anything should happen to you."

"Oh, nonsense, Mother, what power could a creature like that have over me? Besides, I am hungry, and if I don't have my dinner very soon, I shall be cross." And off she went to gather more flowers to add to those already decorating her hair.

About an hour later the blowing of a horn told her that dinner was ready.

"Didn't I say this fish would be delicious?" the girl cried, and, plunging her spoon into the dish, helped herself to a large piece. But the instant it touched her mouth, a cold shiver ran through her. Her head seemed to flatten, and her eyes to look oddly around the corners; her arms were stuck to her sides, and she gasped wildly for breath. With a mighty bound she sprang through the window and fell into the river, where she could breathe more easily, and was able to swim to the sea, which was close by.

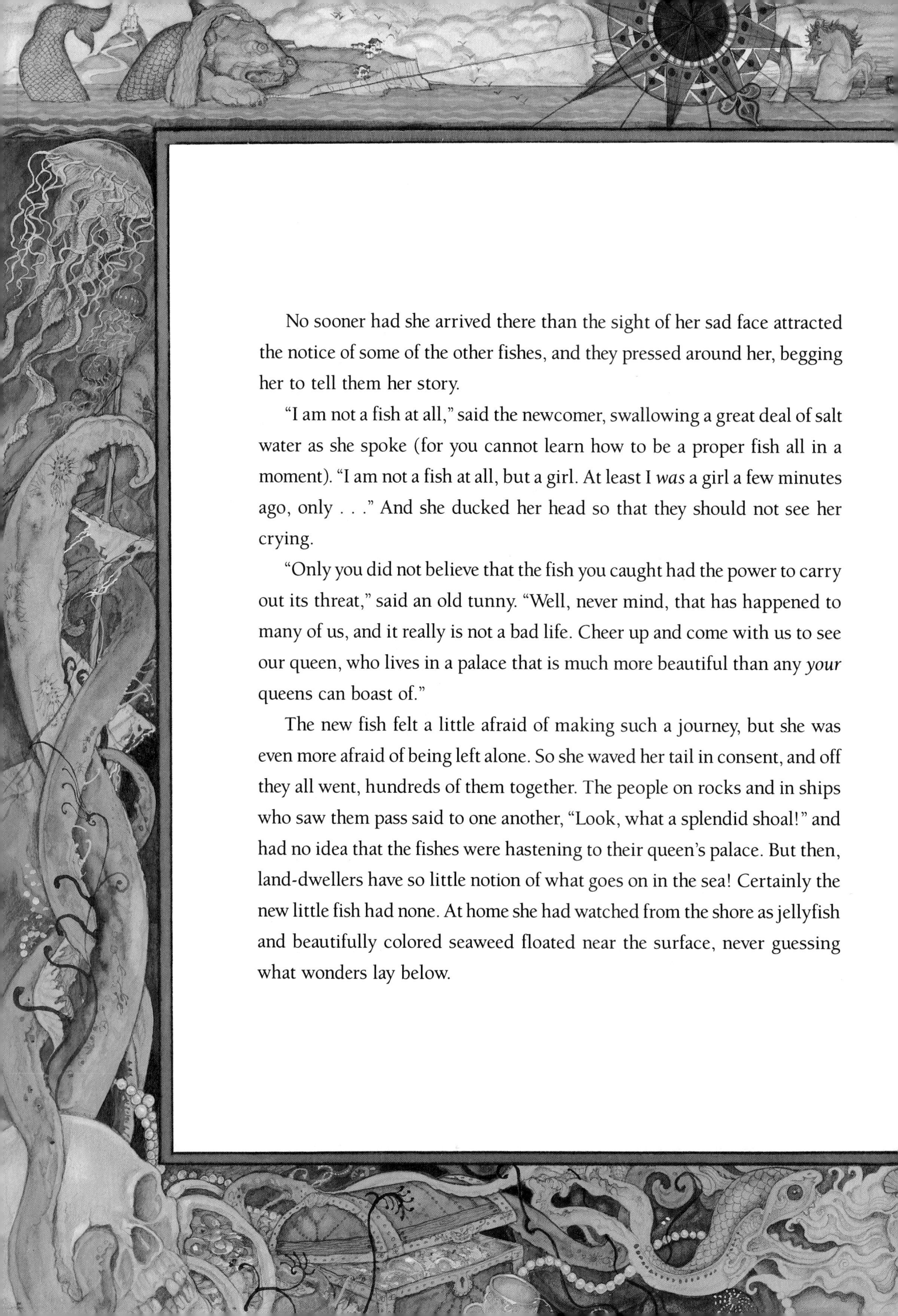

No sooner had she arrived there than the sight of her sad face attracted the notice of some of the other fishes, and they pressed around her, begging her to tell them her story.

"I am not a fish at all," said the newcomer, swallowing a great deal of salt water as she spoke (for you cannot learn how to be a proper fish all in a moment). "I am not a fish at all, but a girl. At least I *was* a girl a few minutes ago, only . . ." And she ducked her head so that they should not see her crying.

"Only you did not believe that the fish you caught had the power to carry out its threat," said an old tunny. "Well, never mind, that has happened to many of us, and it really is not a bad life. Cheer up and come with us to see our queen, who lives in a palace that is much more beautiful than any *your* queens can boast of."

The new fish felt a little afraid of making such a journey, but she was even more afraid of being left alone. So she waved her tail in consent, and off they all went, hundreds of them together. The people on rocks and in ships who saw them pass said to one another, "Look, what a splendid shoal!" and had no idea that the fishes were hastening to their queen's palace. But then, land-dwellers have so little notion of what goes on in the sea! Certainly the new little fish had none. At home she had watched from the shore as jellyfish and beautifully colored seaweed floated near the surface, never guessing what wonders lay below.

But now, when the little fish plunged deeper, strange shapes began to emerge from the green dimness. As first she felt as if she were blind, like the ghostly white creatures she saw living in the cracks of rocks, where the sun's rays never reached. But slowly her eyes adjusted, and the longer she swam—how long, she couldn't tell—the more clearly she saw. And what marvelous things there were to be seen!

Great bars of gold, massive anchors, heaps of pearls, priceless jewels—all scattered at the bottom of the sea along with sunken ships and dead men's bones.

"Here we are at last," cried the big tunny, going down into a deep valley (for the sea has its mountains and valleys just as much as the land). "This is the palace of the queen of the fishes, and is it not as wonderful as I described?"

"It is beautiful indeed," gasped the little fish, who was very tired from trying to swim as fast as the rest. And beautiful beyond words the palace was. The walls were made of pale pink coral, worn smooth by the water, and around the windows were rows of pearls. The great doors were standing open, and the whole troop floated into the audience chamber, where the queen, who was half a woman after all, was seated on a throne made of a green and blue shell.

"Who are you, and where do you come from?" said she to the little fish, whom the others had pushed in front. And in a low, trembling voice, the visitor told her story.

The queen listened intently, compassion in her eyes. "I was once a girl too," she said, when the little fish had ended, "and my father was the king of a great country. A husband was found for me, and on my wedding day my mother placed her crown on my head and told me that as long as I wore it I would likewise be queen. For many seasons I was as happy as a young woman could be, especially after I had a little son. But one morning, when I was walking in my gardens, there came a giant, who snatched the crown from my head. Holding me fast, he told me that he intended to give the crown to his daughter, and would enchant my husband, so that he should not know the difference between us. And she was queen in my stead. I was so miserable that I threw myself into the sea, and my ladies, who loved me, declared that they would die too. But some wizard, who pitied me, turned us all into fishes, though he allowed me to keep something of the face and body of a woman. And fishes we must remain until someone brings me back my crown."

"*I* will bring it back if you tell me what to do!" cried the little fish, who would have promised anything that was likely to carry her up to earth again.

And the queen answered, "Yes, I will tell you what to do."

She sat silent for a moment, and then went on: "You must return to earth, and go up to the top of a high mountain, where the giant has built his castle. You will find him asleep inside, for he has worn himself out with weeping for his daughter, who died while my husband the prince was away hunting. At the last she sent her father my crown by a faithful servant. But I warn you to be careful, for he has a hasty temper and may kill you. Therefore I will give you the power to change yourself into any creature whose skills may help you best. You have only to strike your forehead and call out its name."

The journey to land seemed much shorter than had the one to the palace. When the little fish reached the shore, she struck her forehead sharply with her tail and cried, "Deer, come to me!"

In a moment the small scaly body disappeared, and in its place stood a beautiful beast with branching horns and slender legs, quivering with longing to be gone. Throwing back her head and sniffing the air, the deer broke into a run, leaping over rivers and struggling through thickets that caught at her fur, not stopping once no matter how hard the way.

It happened that the king's son had been hunting since daybreak, but he had killed nothing, and when the deer crossed his path as he was resting under a tree, he was determined to have her. The prince flung himself on his horse, which went like the wind, and as he had often hunted in this forest, he knew all the shortcuts and at last caught up with the panting beast.

"By your favor let me go, and do not kill me," said the deer, turning to the prince with tears in her eyes, "for I have far to run and much to do." And while the prince, struck dumb with surprise, only looked at her, the deer cleared the next stream and was soon out of sight.

"That can't *really* be a deer," thought the prince. "No deer ever had eyes like that. It must be an enchanted maiden, and I will marry her and no other." Then, turning his horse, he rode slowly back to his palace.

The deer, quite out of breath, reached the foot of the mountain which the queen had told her about, and her heart sank as she gazed at the smooth, glasslike surface that stretched up toward the sky. And high on top, barely visible, was perched the giant's castle. But then she plucked up her courage and cried, "Ant, come to me!"

In a moment the branching horns and beautiful shape had vanished, and a tiny brown ant, invisible to all who would not look closely, was climbing up the mountain.

On and on she went, that determined little creature! The mountain appeared as large as the universe itself in comparison with her own body, yet at last she reached the top and was over the wall of the castle and into the courtyard on the other side. Here she paused to consider what to do next. Looking about her, she saw that one of the walls had a tall tree growing by it, and in the corner was a window on a level with the highest branches.

"Monkey, come to me!" cried the ant. And up went an agile monkey, higher and higher. In no time at all she was swinging herself from the topmost branch into the room where the giant lay snoring.

"I had best present myself in a less startling guise," the monkey said to herself, remembering how the queen had warned her about the giant's quick temper. She thought for a moment and then called softly, "Parrot, come to me!"

Then a pink and gray parrot hopped up to the giant, who by this time was stretching himself and giving yawns that shook the castle. The parrot waited a little, until the giant was really awake, and then she said quietly that she had been sent to retrieve the crown, which was his no longer, now that his daughter the false queen was dead.

On hearing these words the giant leaped out of bed with an angry roar and sprang at the parrot, ready to wring her neck with his great hands.

But the bird was too quick for him, and, flying behind his back, said, "I beg you to have patience! My death would be of no use to you."

"By my eyes, that is true," answered the giant roughly, "but I am not so foolish as to give you that crown for nothing. Let me think what I will have in exchange!" And he scratched his huge head for several minutes (for giants' minds always move slowly).

"Ah, yes, that will do!" exclaimed the giant at last, his face brightening. "You shall have the crown if you will bring me a necklace of blue stones from the Arch of Saint Martin, in the Great City."

Now, when the parrot had been a girl, she had often heard of this wonderful arch and the precious stones that decorated it. It sounded as if it would be a very hard thing to pry them from the structure of which they were a part, but she thought of the unhappy queen beneath the sea and resolved that she would try. So the parrot bowed to the giant and flew out the window, where he could not see her. Then she called quickly, "Eagle, come to me!"

At once she felt herself borne up on strong wings ready to carry her to the clouds. Seeming a mere speck in the sky, she swept along over land and sea until she beheld the Arch of Saint Martin sparkling in the sun far below. Then she swooped down and began to dig out the nearest blue stones with her beak. It was even harder work than she had expected, but at last it was done. She drew out a piece of string that she had found hanging from a tree, and carefully, using her mighty talons, strung the stones together. When the necklace was finished, she hung it around her neck and soared upward into the sky and back to the giant's castle. Then she called again, "Parrot, come to me!" and flew inside to stand before the giant.

"Here is the necklace you asked for," said the parrot.

The giant's eyes glistened as he took the string of blue stones in his hand. Yet he was not ready to give up the crown so easily.

"They are hardly as blue as I expected," he grumbled, though the parrot knew as well as he did that he was not speaking the truth. "You must bring me something else in exchange for the crown you covet so much. If you fail, it will cost you not only the crown but your life as well."

The parrot trembled at these words, but again she thought of the poor queen and her ladies. "What is it you want now?" she asked bravely.

The giant answered, "If I give you my crown, I must have another one that is more beautiful still. This time you shall bring me a crown of stars."

The parrot turned away, and as soon as she was outside on the ground, she murmured, "Toad, come to me!" And sure enough a toad she was, and off she jumped in search of a starry crown.

At length she came to a clear pool, in which the stars were reflected so brightly that they looked quite real to touch and hold. She dove in and swam quickly about, using a bag she had carried on her back with which to catch up the stars before the ripples could send them twinkling away. Then, sitting on the bank of the pool, she patiently wove a crown out of the stars, which shone even more brilliantly than those overhead in the night sky.

At daybreak the familiar little figure of the pink and gray parrot stood before the giant.

"Here is the crown you asked for," she said, and this time the giant could not help crying out with admiration. He knew he was beaten; and, holding the chaplet of stars in one hand, he turned to the parrot and gestured to a magnificent cabinet whose doors now lay open.

"Your power is greater than mine. Take your queen's crown—you have won it fairly!"

The parrot did not need to be told twice. Seizing the crown, she sprang to the window and cried joyfully, "Monkey, come to me!" And for a monkey, the climb down the tree into the courtyard was as nothing. Reaching the ground, she said, "Ant, come to me!" And a little ant at once began to crawl down the mountain. How glad that ant was to be away from the giant's castle—and to be holding fast the crown, which had shrunk to almost nothing, as she herself had done, but grew quite big again when the ant exclaimed, "Deer, come to me!"

Surely no deer ever ran so swiftly as that one! On and on she went, bounding over rivers and crashing through thickets until finally she reached the sea. Here she cried, "Fish, come to me!" And with a mighty leap, the enchanted fish that so long ago had been a selfish, carefree child, splashed into the sea and swam along the bottom to the palace, where the queen and all the fishes were gathered together awaiting her.

"I am tired of staying here," grumbled a beautiful little creature whose colors changed with every movement of her body. "I want to see what is going on in the upper world. It must be *years* since that fish went away!"

"It was a very difficult task, and the giant must certainly have killed her or she would have been back long ago," remarked another.

"The young flies will be coming out now," murmured a third, "and they will all be eaten up by the river fishes! It is really *too* bad!"

Suddenly a fourth fish called out, "Look! Look! What is that bright thing that is moving so swiftly toward us?"

The queen started up, and stood on her tail, so excited was she.

Silence fell on all the crowd, and even the grumblers held their peace and gazed like the rest. Gliding through the water came the little fish, holding the crown tightly in her mouth, and the others moved back to let her pass. On she went right up to the queen, who bent and, taking the crown, placed it on her own head. Then a wonderful thing happened. The queen's tail dropped away—or, rather, it divided and grew into two legs and a pair of the prettiest feet in the world, while her ladies, who were grouped around her, shed their scales and became human again. They all turned and looked first at one another, and next at the little fish, who had regained her human shape and was now a young woman, more beautiful than all the rest.

"It is *you* who has given us back our life—*you, you!*" they cried, and fell to weeping with joy.

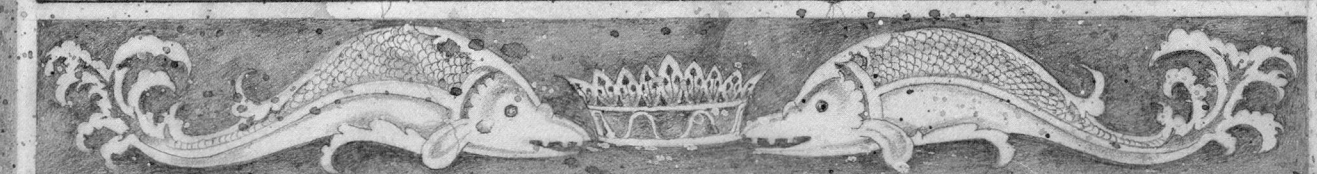

So they all went back to earth and the queen's earthly palace. But they had been so long away that they found many changes. The queen's husband had died some years ago, and in his place was her son, who had grown up and was king. Even in his joy at seeing his mother again, an air of sadness clung to him. At last the queen could bear it no longer, and begged him to walk with her in the garden. Seated with him in a bower of jasmine—where she had passed long hours as a bride—she took her son's hand and entreated him to tell her the cause of his sorrow. "For," said she, "if I can give you happiness, you shall have it."

"It is no use," answered the prince. "Nobody can help me. I must bear it alone."

"But at least let me share your grief," urged the queen.

"No one can do that," said he. "I have fallen in love with what I can never marry, and I must get on as best I can."

"It may not be so impossible as you think," answered the queen. "At any rate, tell me."

There was silence between them for a moment. Then, turning his head away, the prince said quietly, "Some time ago I was hunting in the forest, and there I fell in love with a beautiful deer!"

"Ah, if *that* is all!" exclaimed the queen joyfully. And she told him that, as he had guessed, it was no deer he had seen but an enchanted maiden. "The very one," added the queen, "who won back my crown and brought me home to my people. She is here, in my palace. I will take you to her."

But when the prince stood before the young woman, who was so much more beautiful than anything he had ever dreamed of, he lost his courage, and stood with bent head before her.

Then the maiden drew near, and her eyes, as she looked up at him, were the eyes of the deer that day in the forest. She whispered softly, "By your favor let me go, and do not kill me."

The prince remembered her words, and his heart was filled with happiness. And the queen, his mother, watched them and smiled.

Concealed in the final illustration, readers can find each of the animals depicted in the story: the parrot, fish, deer, eagle, toad, ant, and monkey.

A Note on the Text

The Girl, the Fish, and the Crown is adapted from *The Girl-Fish* by Dr. D. Francisco de S. Maspons y Labros in *Cuentos Populars Catalans*. An English translation was published in preeminent folklorist Andrew Lang's *Orange Fairy Book*.

VIKING
Published by the Penguin Group
Penguin Books USA Inc., 375 Hudson Street, New York, New York 10014, U.S.A.
Penguin Books Ltd, 27 Wrights Lane, London W8 5TZ, England
Penguin Books Australia Ltd, Ringwood, Victoria, Australia
Penguin Books Canada Ltd, 10 Alcorn Avenue, Toronto, Ontario, Canada M4V 3B2
Penguin Books (N.Z.) Ltd, 182–190 Wairau Road, Auckland 10, New Zealand

Penguin Books Ltd, Registered Offices: Harmondsworth, Middlesex, England

First published in 1995 by Viking, a division of Penguin Books USA Inc.

1 3 5 7 9 10 8 6 4 2

Copyright © Marilee Heyer, 1995

LIBRARY OF CONGRESS CATALOGING-IN-PUBLICATION DATA
Heyer, Marilee.
The girl, the fish & the crown / Marilee Heyer.   p.   cm.
Summary: While on a dangerous quest which requires her to take the form of different
wild animals, a selfish young girl learns about compassion and generosity.
ISBN 0-670-85409-3
[1. Folklore—Spain.] I. Title. II. Title: Girl, the fish, and the crown.
PZ8.1.H49Gi 1995 398.2'094601—dc20 [E] 94-42793 CIP AC

Printed in Singapore
Set in Berkeley Oldstyle